TERROR
in
BEAR
CANYON

Written by Robert Charles

Illustrated by Brian Harrison

TERROR in BEAR CANYON

Contents

Chapter 1
Bear Canyon. 4

Chapter 2
The Rattler 9

Chapter 3
The Water Hole 15

Chapter 4
Noises in the Night 21

Chapter 5
Bear Alert 27

Chapter 6
Running the Rapids. 35

Chapter 7
Rock Fall. 39

Chapter 8
Don't Look Down 43

CHAPTER 1
Bear Canyon

Jason and Jack stood at the south rim of Bear Canyon and looked down deep into the gorge below.

"Wow!" breathed Jack as he looked down the steep canyon walls to the bottom. "What a magnificent sight! It's all I thought it would be and more."

"The river looks just like a little sleepy, slithering snake down there," said Jason. "A sleepy snake right in the middle of brown bear country!"

Jason and Jack had been planning their trip to Bear Canyon all winter. They liked facing challenges and Bear Canyon was a big challenge. It was steep and rugged and the trails were narrow. It was also the home of rattlesnakes and bears.

The brothers had read up on canyon wildlife even though they knew that the chances of seeing a snake or a bear were pretty slim. Each year, many hikers were injured in Bear Canyon, especially those who did not respect the wildlife and did not know basic safety rules. Most of them could have avoided the dangerous situations they put themselves in.

"Let's go," said Jason, checking to make sure that they had more than enough water to get them to Snake River.

They were not more than two hours into their hike when they came across their first challenge. In their way was a snake and it was a rattler.

"It could be longer than you if it wasn't coiled up, Jason," said Jack in a hushed voice. "I wish it wasn't here."

"Me too," said Jason, because the snake had chosen to sun itself on the only path that led to the bottom of the canyon. There was absolutely no way around.

To make matters worse, the rattlesnake didn't look like it was going to move, and by the way it was shaking its rattle, it was not in the best of moods. In fact it was clearly telling the brothers to stay well away.

"Oh no!" said Jack. "I really don't think this snake likes us. This is not a good way to start our hike. The first day out and we run into a bad-tempered rattlesnake."

"It won't hurt us if we ignore it," replied Jason. "It's not hunting for food. Anyway we're much too big to be a rattlesnake's dinner, it could never swallow us."

But Jack was not so sure.

"What are we going to do now?" he asked quietly, still staring at the rattlesnake.

Jason just shrugged his shoulders, but he was starting to formulate a plan.

CHAPTER 2
The Rattler

"I'll see if I can frighten it away," replied
Jason, and this is where he made his first silly
mistake of the trip. He began shuffling his feet
in the loose gravel on the path, but the snake
did not move away. Instead it raised its head
higher as though it was about to strike.

"Get back, Jason," yelled Jack, as the snake
began to move.

Jason didn't need to be told twice, he quickly
backed off to a safer distance

Jack was now starting to get angry with his brother.

"Any other bright ideas, Señor Snake Charmer?" he said sarcastically.

"Yeah, stand back and watch this," responded Jason fearlessly. Then he made another silly mistake.

"This'll move it," he said and he began to toss small rocks at the snake.

But the snake still did not move an inch, in fact, it became even more irritated. It raised its head high, showed its fangs, and then suddenly struck out in the direction of where Jason and Jack were standing.

Even though they were out of the snake's reach, the brothers both jumped back quickly, bumping each other.

"Look out!" shrieked Jack angrily. "You almost knocked me over."

"Sorry," replied Jason sheepishly. "I guess I got a fright. I thought the snake would move off when I threw the stones at it, I didn't think it would strike."

While they were talking the snake slowly slithered into the rocks just off the path.

"Look, it's going," said Jason with relief. "Let's get past before it decides to come out for more."

Jason cautiously moved on down the path and past the spot where the snake had been coiled and had crawled into the rocks. The he turned around and smiled an encouraging smile at Jack.

"See, it's OK," he said. "Now come on before Ratty Rattler decides to come out of the rocks and get all unfriendly again."

Now it was Jack's turn to get past the rocks where the snake was hiding. He knew he had to summon up the courage because there was no other way, and they had to move on down the path to the watering spot at Snake River before the day got any hotter.

"Come on, Jack," Jason encouraged him, "It's OK. The snake's gone. Come on."

Shaking like a leaf, Jack hustled down the path. Just as he got to the spot where the snake was hiding he heard Jason yell.

"Look out, Jack!" Jason screamed.

But it was too late. As Jason screamed the rattlesnake shot out of the rocks like a missile, its mouth stretched wide and its deadly fangs poised for attack.

Jack sprang forward, terror written all over his face. But as he jumped, he lost his footing and fell. The rattler's venomous fangs seemed to graze his leg as the loose rocks gave way under his hiking boots. His knees buckled under him and he slumped, panic-stricken, to the ground as the snake slithered back into the rocks.

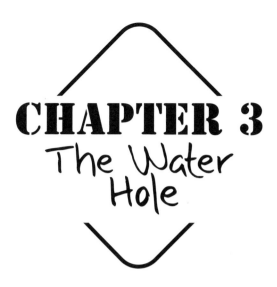

CHAPTER 3
The Water Hole

Jason quickly reached out, grabbed Jack's outstretched hand, and pulled him roughly to his feet.

"Come on!" he yelled as he half lifted, half dragged a frightened Jack down the trail to where it was safe. "We can't stop until we get well away from that rattler. We have to keep going. Now come on, Jack. Try and help yourself."

"I'm going to die," Jack panted, terror still blanketing his face. "That snake bit my leg. I know I'm going to die."

"No you're not," replied Jason, although he didn't feel very confident about things at all. He knew only too well that you shouldn't move people who have been bitten by snakes, but he needed to get his brother away from danger, so he had no other option. "It's safe now," he continued as he stopped running. "Let me look at your leg."

He bent down and Jack heard him breathe a sigh of relief.

"The snake missed your leg," Jason said. "There are absolutely no fang marks at all, just a surface graze from the rocks. You're going to be just fine, so take a little rest and have a drink of water and when the shock wears off we'll get going again."

Jack looked down at his grazed leg, still expecting to see fang marks. It felt like jelly, but then so did his other leg.

"OK," he said shakily, "we do need to get going, because it's at least three hours to the watering station and we don't want to run out of water before we get there."

"You're right," agreed Jason. "We do still have a lot of ground to cover."

As Jason spoke, Jack got shakily to his feet and they started off again. Although they were walking downhill, the weight of their backpacks began to take its toll and they both began to sweat profusely.

"We'd better go easy on the water," said Jack as he stopped and took a sip. "We'll have to ration it if we don't make good time, and that will not be a good scene in this heat."

"Right," said Jason, smiling. "If we get delayed by another bad-tempered rattlesnake we could be in serious trouble without water."

"Don't even mention the word snake to me," Jack shot back. "I've had my fill of snakes. One more encounter with a ratty rattler and I'm turning around and heading out of this canyon as fast as my legs will take me."

After that the brothers hiked in silence for a while, stopping occasionally to sip their water and nibble on their trail mix.

"We're here," said Jack, breaking the silence as they reached the watering spot, "and it looks like we made it here just in time. If it had taken us any longer, we would have run right out of water."

"Let's rest here for a couple of hours," said Jason. "It's as good a place as any to eat lunch. I don't know about you, but I'm hungry enough to eat a snake."

"Jason!" Jack said threateningly.

"OK, OK," Jason replied. "I'm just teasing. You really are very sensitive about that old rattlesnake aren't you?"

Jack didn't bother to reply.

They found a shady spot, took off their backpacks and took out the fruit and sandwiches they had packed for lunch.

When they finished eating, they lay down and raised their legs to get the blood moving to the upper part of their bodies. Within minutes they were both sound asleep.

When they awoke an hour and a half later the sun had begun to drop in the western sky.

"We better hit the trail quickly if we hope to reach the camp ground before dark," Jack said. "Sunset is at 8 o'clock and we still have five hours of hiking ahead of us. We certainly don't want to be setting up our tent in the dark."

"Let's hit the road then," said Jason, picking up his pack and leading the way on down the trail.

CHAPTER 4
Noises in the Night

Jack and Jason reached the campsite half an hour before sunset.

"This is just perfect," Jack said. "Perfect timing and a perfect place."

The campsite was nestled in a small valley where a stream gurgled down from high above on the canyon rim. The stream supplied water for large cottonwood trees and many smaller shrubs and bushes.

"You're right, Jack, this is a perfect place to spend the night," said Jason.

Little did he know what lay ahead.

The brothers quickly set up their camp and gathered some wood. With the tent erected and sleeping bags laid out, it was time to build a fire and prepare something for their evening meal.

The temperature was beginning to drop as the sky darkened. There was not a cloud in the sky as the sun slipped slowly and silently over the horizon. Jack was always impressed by the way stars seemed to pop out of the evening sky as it got darker and darker.

"They look just like sparkling jewels," he said as he looked upward in amazement.

"Jewels?" asked Jason, puzzled, not knowing what Jack was talking about.

"Diamonds," replied Jack. "The stars out here twinkle just like diamonds."

"Enough about diamonds and jewels. Let's eat," said Jason. "I'm hungry again."

After dinner, they sat around the fire talking about their first day in Bear Canyon. Then they started to talk about the preparations for the next day. They talked for what seemed like hours.

Finally Jason looked at his watch and they decided that it was time to turn in. He poured water over the fire and kicked dirt over the ashes.

They both washed their faces and brushed their teeth in the stream and then they crawled into the tent and climbed into their sleeping bags. It was warm and cosy in the tent and within seconds they were both out like lights.

Suddenly, Jack woke with a start and sat bolt upright trying to work out where he was.

Then he remembered that he and Jason were camping in Bear Canyon. But what could possibly have woken him?

Jack strained his ears but he could hear nothing. What time was it? How long had he been asleep? It was still very dark so he looked at his watch and was surprised to see that it was three o'clock.

Then he heard a noise – it was an odd shuffling sound. He couldn't identify it, but he was already starting to feel frightened.

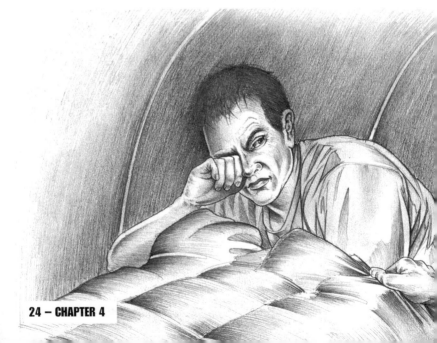

What if it was another rattlesnake?

Jack nudged Jason awake. "Can you hear that noise?" he whispered urgently. "It sounds like something's out there."

Jason sat up, rubbed his sleepy eyes and listened. Then he realized what Jack was saying.

"Oh no!" he gasped, suddenly aware that he had made yet another very silly mistake, "I forgot to tie up the food!"

"Are you saying what I think you're saying?" whispered Jack even more urgently, his heart banging around in his chest like a herd of wild elephants.

Jason slowly nodded his head up and down.

"Yes," he replied. "I think the only thing that's separating us from a couple of big brown bears is a thin layer of canvas."

"What are we going to do?" asked Jack.

CHAPTER 5
Bear Alert

Carefully, quietly, and very tentatively, Jason lifted the tent flap up a bit. Sure enough, right outside the tent were two enormous brown bears feasting on the food that he had forgotten to tie up. Quickly Jason dropped the tent flap back down.

"There's nothing we can do," he said to Jack. "We'll just have to keep still and hope they don't come any nearer the tent."

The brothers lay there in the dark like statues, hardly daring to breathe. It seemed that they lay there forever.

In fact, it was only ten minutes before the bears finished all of the food and wandered off into the darkness without taking a closer look at the tent.

Jack and Jason both breathed long, slow sighs of relief.

"That was nothing short of a miracle," said Jack, "now let's get out of here before they come back. We've been lucky to escape so far, so let's not tempt fate any further."

In no time at all, Jack and Jason had packed up the tent and the small amount of food that the bears had left after their feast.

"We're not going to have too much to eat for the rest of the trip," said Jason, wishing that he had taken proper precautions. "But at least we still have the dried food that was in the tent."

"I'm beginning to think we should have stayed home," said Jack as they set off into the night. "We've been gone less than 24 hours and we've already had two close encounters with danger. Let's hope we're getting all the bad stuff over with early."

Seven long hours later, Jason and Jack reached the bottom of the canyon. They had walked through the night and into the dawn and by now all Jason could think of was the cool waters of the Snake River.

Jack, however, was not too keen on jumping into any river with "snake" in its name. "Why do they call it Snake River?" he asked Jason.

"Because it's filled with big old slithering ratty rattlesnakes," joked Jason.

"Very funny," retorted Jack. "Be serious can't you? If there is even one snake in that river I would rather roast to death in this heat than get into the water."

"The only reason they call it Snake River is because it snakes through the canyon like a lazy snake," said Jason. "So come on. Take off your hiking boots and get into the water. You won't believe how refreshing it is."

Jack took off his hiking boots, emptied his pockets, and joined Jason in the cool refreshing water of the Snake River.

"You're right, Jason, it feels like a million dollars," he said. "Now let's get dry. We're short of food, remember?"

But Jason made yet another silly mistake. Instead of staying near the bank, he swam into the middle of the river without checking the flow of the water and he was soon caught up in a swift current and began drifting down the river.

He swam frantically against the current but couldn't fight his way out. He tried swimming across the current to get to the far bank but the river was just too strong for him.

Jack could see what was happening and for the third time since they had started out, he was frightened. First the snake, then the bears, and now this.

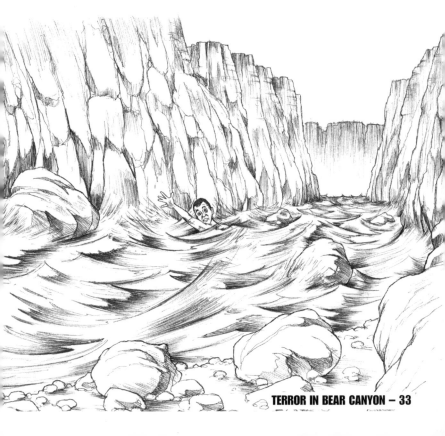

He quickly clambered out of the water and ran along the river's edge, hoping with all his heart that he would be able to find a way to help Jason. As he looked down the river he could see white-water rapids churning up the water and making it look as though it was boiling.

He knew if Jason got sucked into the rapids that could be the end of him. But what could he do? Jason was too far from shore to reach.

So Jack did the only thing he could. He shouted as loud as he possibly could, "Rapids ahead! Swim for your life!"

CHAPTER 6
Running the Rapids

Jason swam as hard as he could, but he couldn't escape the pull of the river. Within seconds he was tumbling through the raging rapids. He struggled to keep his head above water.

"How could I have escaped the bears only to be caught in this?" he thought as he dropped into a churning hole of wild water and went under.

He still had not realized that it was his own stupidity that was creating unnecessary problems for them.

But then, suddenly, as if another miracle had occurred, the churning water spat Jason out and deposited him face down on a large rock near the bank of the river. The fall knocked the wind out of him, but at least he was finally free of the raging torrent.

"Jason! Jason!" Jack shouted, rushing as fast as he could to where Jason lay.

By the time Jack got to him, Jason was spitting water and coughing. Jack, still alarmed, asked Jason if he was all right.

Then suddenly Jason started to laugh with relief. "What a ride!" he said. "Am I lucky?"

"You must have had the good luck fairy sitting on your shoulder while you were in the river," Jack said, a smile slowly spreading from ear to ear. "Now let's get back to our backpacks and eat."

Jack mixed a dried chicken and rice dinner with plenty of cool water and let it soak. He thought that the water would at least soften the rice grains and make the chicken moist so it would go down easier.

"We'll need lots of water to wash this down," Jason said, making a face a the chicken and rice dinner. "It's very dry. Perhaps that's why the bears didn't come into the tent to steal it."

"Do you think the bears would have come back if we had stayed there?" asked Jack.

"I'm sure of it," Jason replied.

After dinner they discussed their plans for hiking out of the canyon the next day.

"We could retrace our steps and return by way of the south rim trail," Jason said. "Or we could go with the original plan."

"Why don't we stick with the original plan?" suggested Jack, not wanting further encounters with snakes and bears. "If we get an early start, we might be able to hike out in one day. I'd prefer that."

"It'll be a long day," said Jason. "So let's hit the sack now."

CHAPTER 7
Rock Fall

Morning came around pretty quickly. Jason and Jack were up well before sunrise, all ready to start their final day's hike.

Jack was eager to get started. His spirits were high and he couldn't wait to be hiking again.

After breakfast they loaded up with fresh water, packed their backpacks and headed up the north rim trail on the way out of Bear Canyon.

The hike out was going smoothly and they were only two hours from the north rim where they would find soft beds, warm food and hot showers. But then disaster struck again!

It happened as they were hiking along a narrow part of the trail with the steep canyon walls rising above them. They heard a loud rumbling sound from above and looked up to see a large rock fragment that had broken loose tumbling toward them.

Jason hugged the canyon wall as tightly as possible. Jack, on the other hand, scrambled to get out of the way.

But in his haste, Jack lost his footing and started to slide. The rock hit the trail where they had been standing, bounced high into the air and caught Jack as it bounced on down the canyon.

"Help!" he screamed as he lost his balance completely and teetered off the edge of the trail.

CHAPTER 8
Don't Look Down

"Jack! NO!" Jason screamed a blood-curdling scream as he rushed to the place where Jack had disappeared. He was almost too afraid to look over the edge because he felt sure that he would see Jack's crumpled body way down on the canyon floor. There was no way anyone could have possibly survived such a fall.

"Jack! Jack!" he yelled again as his eyes frantically searched below. And then he saw Jack, but he was not on the canyon floor – he was clinging to a small tree not too far below where he stood.

"Hang on, Jack," he shouted. "I'll get you out. Whatever you do, don't let go."

He got down on his stomach, stretched his right arm and hand as far as he could and tried to take hold of Jack's hand to pull him up.

But try as hard as he could and stretch as far
as he could, Jason couldn't quite reach Jack.

"Hang on just a bit longer," Jason called out.
"I'll have to get something for you to grab."

"Hurry," Jack cried, his voice now full of alarm and agitation. "I don't think I can hold on much longer."

Jason ran around looking for a branch or anything to extend his reach but he found nothing. Then it suddenly occurred to him that he had long overpants in his backpack.

He quickly grabbed the overpants out of his backpack and lowered one end of them down to Jack. "Grab my pants!" he yelled, "and hold on tight as I pull you out."

"I can't," Jack replied.

"You have to," yelled Jason. "Don't say you can't. Just grab hold of them one hand at a time. You can do it, but whatever you do, Jack, don't look down."

Jack took a deep breath and slowly released his grip on the tree and with one hand, reached up and grabbed Jason's pants. Then he grabbed hold of the pants with his other hand and held on for dear life.

Jason felt Jack's weight and started to pull him up. It was hard work and Jason felt as though his arms were being pulled clean away from the rest of his body, but he gritted his teeth and pulled and pulled and pulled.

Then just as he hauled Jack, shaking but safe, back onto the trail, Jason heard a friendly female voice.

"Are you hurt?" she asked.

Jack and Jason looked up to see the park ranger.

"Just grazed and thankful to be safe," replied Jack.

"Are you just starting out?" the ranger asked.

"No way," replied Jack, getting up. "I've had enough of Bear Canyon to last me a lifetime. We've had nothing but bad luck since we arrived." And with that he recounted to the ranger all the things that had happened to them.

"Sounds more like bad management and stupidity than bad luck," the ranger said when Jack had finished his story. "People like you two should do your planning more thoroughly. You're both extremely lucky to be alive."